He Stepped Out of the Taxi...

COLIN W SLATER

He Stepped Out Of The Taxi...

First Published 2025.

Revised 2025.

Copyright © 2025 Colin W Slater.

Edited by Stuart W Slater.

Contributions by Stuart W Slater.

ISBN: 978-1-0369-1384-7

Prologue

"Did you like that story?" David asked.

"We did, Grandad. We all did! Your journey from boy to man. Your first job and how nervous you felt. It was wonderful. Did you make it up, or was it true?"

David was heart warmed by the genuine responses.

"Do you remember," he replied, "I told you all there would come a day, a time, when I would become too old to recall my real adventures, and I would have to invent stories for you? Maybe that day has come. What do you think?"

"You will never be old, Grandad," the children chorused.

"Was the story true? Do tell us what happened next? What happened after you stepped out of the taxi?"

David Winters's three children were now grown up with their own families. He had been blessed with a loving family who visited him every Friday, enabling him to stay connected with their world, and they with world events. He would ask them, in turn, to share something they had learned each week that they did not know before. As far as the children were concerned—and of much more interest to them—was that after they had finished their meal, Grandad would tell what he called one of his 'adventures'.

It was that time now.

Grandad looked proudly around the well-furnished room, smiled, and asked, "Everyone warm enough? It's a bit nippy in here tonight." He leaned across the tiled hearth and used a long iron poker to revive the fire. A few embers began to glow again as he laid two logs gently on top.

"They'll soon burn," he said reassuringly.

"Come on, Grandad, another story, please!" a voice pleaded. The children looked hopefully at their dad and beamed with joy when he nodded permission with happy approval.

They settled into more comfortable positions.

"OK," David said, "One more story. Let me see. Shall I tell you about when I was Captain of the submarine Atlanta and how I prevented a world catastrophe?"

"You've already told us that one!" laughed the children.

"Ah! Right." David winked.

"Did I tell you when I drove a stagecoach from York to London?"

"Yes! And it was London to York!" shouted the granddaughter. Her eyes sparkled with playful defiance, arms now crossed as she challenged him to remember correctly.

"Oh, yes, so I did. You're right." He chuckled, rubbing the back of his neck. Glancing at her, his eyes warmed with nostalgia. She grinned.

"But, Grandad, you haven't answered the question," interrupted another. "What happened after you stepped out of the taxi?"

2

"Good point," conceded David. "The old memory is not what it was. Let me see now. Oh yes, I remember, the taxi drove away, and I stood awhile, determining there and then to make a real success of my life—as I hope you all will. I worked long hours, took on more responsibility, was promoted through the ranks, and eventually held a senior position. However, I began to tire of the constant pressure that came with the role. My children were all but grown up, and I needed a new direction in my life. I needed some excitement, something daring-do. But what? I thought, should I go to France and join the French Foreign Legion? Then I remembered I couldn't speak French, didn't like sand in my boots, couldn't stand being ordered about, or running for miles in the sun."

The children laughed.

"So I underwent training at Beechwood Manor and became an Intelligence Officer in the service of Her Majesty, responsible for Eastern Europe and Russian operations. I was given a safe house in Malta, where I lived for a while."

He looked at the children.

"Shall I go on?"

"Yes, please!" the children replied enthusiastically.

"Well, it's a story where I tracked down, unmasked, and arrested a Russian agent working in MI6."

He looked at them again.

"It's a long story. Are you sure?"

They nodded eagerly, leaning forward with anticipation.

He had the response he wanted, so he moved closer and lowered his voice. His expression grew serious.

"In which case, I think it's wise to change my name and the names of my fellow operatives to protect their identities."

His gaze lingered on each of them as if gauging their trust.

"I was on an operation in East Germany and had word that my friend and associate, Jack, had discovered the identity of a mole—that's a spy. I was sent in to contact Jack and bring him back. I made my way to the rendezvous point and peered through the narrow window above the courtyard, just in time to see some movement in the shadows below. What I did not know was that plans were being made to ambush and eliminate Jack."

The children held their breath, eyes wide. One whispered, "What happened next?"

"I knew then that we had a 'stranger', a traitor, in our midst. I set out to find out who that traitor was. Jack knew and was about to tell me, but then he couldn't. He was silenced."

The children gasped. They knew what that meant.

"What happened next must remain a secret," David said, looking around the room. They all slowly and seriously nodded in agreement.

"Good," he said.

"Well, I watched through a gap in the curtain as events unfolded..."

CHAPTER ONE
Betrayal

East Germany.

Jack drove into the courtyard, and his damaged car came to a dead stop. They were nearly on him. The beating he had received a few hours earlier was clouding his clarity of thought. Sweat stung his eyes as he looked around, desperate to find a way out. He urgently needed to create a distraction. Stretching across the front seat, he kicked open the passenger door and, seizing their momentary hesitation, dove through, arms and head first.

Even before he had a chance to make for the dark of the alley, they had regained the initiative. He arched his back the instant he heard the bullet leave the barrel, but it had already pierced his skin and entered his shoulder on its way to shattering the bone. He groaned with the pain.

The speed of the bullet pushed at him as, in the same split second, he twisted his body a full ninety degrees and flung himself away. No sooner had he hit the ground and slid beside the back of his crumpled car than two more shots ricocheted off the pavement, screeching past his prone, motionless form. He rolled over, inching forward to make the best use of angles for cover. Expert, repetitive training and sheer desperation for survival made Jack Donaldson's actions more or less involuntary.

5

He had known this outcome was likely since word came that Trueman, a senior intelligence officer, had gone to Qatar. Neither of them understood why the orders had been given. Trueman had said it was too soon, that they were not ready. Jack was a first-class operative—perhaps the best. But in uncovering the truth, he had sealed his own fate.

Two days earlier, in London, the Controller had received a request for an immediate, strictly personal collection. He declined, judging it unnecessary and risky. Jack had been a little too obvious—not his usual style. However, the events that followed transpired with such speed and ruthless determination that there was little chance of avoiding the ultimate consequence of betrayal.

On the second floor of the austere East German hotel, overlooking the ensuing scene, Deputy Controller David Stewart pressed the phone to his ear, leaned hard against the wall adjacent to the window, and eased the curtain just enough to see but not enough to let light escape. Gingerly, he leant forward and scanned the area below with foreboding— not only for Jack but also for the inevitability of what was soon to happen.

Jack and David were not just British Intelligence operatives; they were friends. They had both been contemporaries at Beechwood Manor, from where they both graduated with distinction over a decade ago.

It was Jack who had encouraged and supported David through difficult moments. Jack found it easy. For David, it had been a tough eighteen months. On their last morning, two cars waited on the sweeping gravel driveway as they exited the dark-panelled hall. Night gave way as the sky stretched awake and gave light to the two journeys about to begin.

The Queen's Oath had secured loyalty to country; handshakes sealed loyalty to each other. It was a loyalty not spoken—but even more binding. Only the reserved English, with their unwritten constitution and long tradition of meaningful knowing silences, could fully understand and mean it. Jack took David's arm, congratulated him warmly, and shook his hand with a firm grip. David knew what it meant—a secret shared.

Memories of their time at Beechwood ebbed and flowed through his mind. Submerged emotions breached his inner defences. He had forgotten how to feel. But for a brief moment, he once again tasted excitement, pride and duty—a mixture of bravery and bravado, a dash of fear, and a generous splash of the unknown.

Fourteen painful, rarely pleasant, or satisfying years had taught him that life was different. The journey quickly dented his eagerness and anticipation before demolishing them completely. Little about the seedy side of man's deceit, greed, and brutality was unknown to him.

7

The noise from below caught David's immediate attention. The attack on Jack was the confirming, concluding act. The information had been impeccable: the place, the time, even the method. Only the obvious attention it was bound to attract—indeed, was attracting—troubled David. He pushed the thought aside for another time.

David vigorously shook the phone, hoping for clearer reception, then pressed it back to his ear. The line still crackled. He felt unsure and decided to give only the briefest outline.

"Listen," the familiar voice of George Robbins said. "Instructions from the Controller. Jack is going to be taken. Return to London ASAP. Do it. End of discussion." David pressed the 'off' button and angrily pushed the phone back into his side pocket. He had been overruled.

Pulling himself upright, he slowly closed the narrow gap in the curtains created moments before. Jack was his comrade, and he knew there were no alternatives, no scope for discretion or manoeuvre. Jack was totally committed; he would understand. Even knowing all this, what David was going to do—and what he had to do—didn't ease the dreadful ache of guilt and despair that hit the pit of his stomach. David was tired, dirty, and disenchanted. He understood only too well that, as many times in the past, he would have to kill to survive.

The occupant of the hotel room, a bespectacled man of Mediterranean complexion and small stature, lay naked on the king-sized bed. He was unmarked but unmistakably dead. Next to him, also naked, lay his passion: a pretty blonde, probably in her late twenties, though with the entrapping look of being younger. They had been dead when David arrived. The afterlife was no longer a mystery to either of them.

David had discovered she used her youthful appearance and body to plant the seed that led Trueman to Malta and David to that particular room that particular night. He needed to find the connection. And quickly.

He left the room, closing the door silently behind, and edged across the brightly lit passage. Moving swiftly down the stairway, he exited through the window he had wedged open earlier for precisely that purpose. It had taken no more than six minutes. The waiting car pulled closer. He climbed in and leaned back on the freshly cleaned leather. The events of the last week raced in his mind, but he was still not sure. Police sirens sounded loudly and grew nearer as he was driven briskly away.

Two days later, David Stewart shifted into a more restful position and gazed idly out of the aircraft window. He watched as the clouds occasionally parted, revealing fleeting glimpses of the land below.

He had made a promise to find those who betrayed Jack. It was his duty to his country, but for David, it was more than that—it was a duty to Jack. It was deeply personal. He was determined to seek revenge, justice, or both. If not the latter, then *definitely* the former.

A gentle voice and a soft touch on his arm drew him back to the present. A smiling stewardess reminded him to fasten his seatbelt. "We'll be landing shortly, sir." She moved along the narrow aisle, repeating the request to other passengers. The landing was smooth, and the tannoy announcement instructed everyone to remain seated until the plane came to a complete stop.

He made his way through airport control and customs. "Welcome to Athens," the customs official said, his expression glum, his tone disinterested. "Just the one bag, Mr... er...?"

"Cummings." David Stewart interrupted quickly.

"Yes." The official repeated the question while glancing between David and the photograph in the passport. "What is the purpose of your visit, Mr. Cummings? Business or pleasure?"

"Pleasure," David replied with a smile.

He reached his car, slipped it into gear, and drove quickly away.

CHAPTER TWO
The Body

Anglesey, North Wales.

Moelfre on the Isle of Anglesey, separated from the rest of Wales by two bridges, was a notorious area and haven for smugglers. It was considered a model example of a quiet harbour town. Even the visitors it attracted were usually the more staid and mature type, not given to outbursts of loutish behaviour or the odd spot of GBH. Over-reliance on this view gave rise to the also optimistic proposition that, as there had been no major crime for many years, why should that state of affairs not continue?

The police station was located on the west side of the harbour, prominently situated adjacent to the doctor's surgery. Combining two or more public uses in a single building was a common feature of the time. It was sometimes considered, usually correctly, to make economic and practical sense, particularly in small communities. Despite a vigorous campaign some four years earlier, the station had been closed and sold under a 'Regional Rationalisation' programme following the Harrison Report. Home Office accountants had easily won the debate in the process of ring-fencing capital receipts from the sale of assets, often with a consequent reduction in ongoing revenue.

11

This was carried out in the face of fierce opposition and against the well-organised, vocal demands of the local residents. It was not a popular decision. Fears were even expressed that the lack of a visible police presence would affect tourism, a major source of income. The authorities, experienced in such matters, however, knew that over time, memories can be fickle, and a sudden influx of visitors over the summer months meant the anger would be short-lived. The building was now a sought-after, upmarket hotel and restaurant, which offered, according to the brochure, 'inmate private candlelit dining in cosy individual rooms.' The missing 'ti' had originally been a misprint, but the owners chose to leave it on all promotional material after realising it had given the Soft Cell Hotel celebrity status.

They had even changed the menu to profitable effect, offering such delights as *Apple Pie with Custody*, *Handcuffed Pies topped with File-o-Pastry*, and *Locally-Court-Poached Salmon* with *Sarge and Onion Stuffing*. These went down well with the locals.

The reduction in police numbers and reallocation of resources to inner-city Wales was either perfectly justified and inspired thinking, or it was naive and short-sighted. History would judge in the long term. In the short term, events were already overtaking hope.

Constable Owen Baker paced impatiently back and forth, troubled not only by what had occurred but also by the thought of the additional workload ahead.

The sun's rays pierced the window and reached the silver frame on his desk, partly obscuring the photograph of his wife and two children. He picked it up, polished it against his uniform sleeve, and quietly spoke to his wife in the picture, rehearsing what he knew he had to say. "Sorry, love. I know you hate being in the house alone at night, but it looks like this is how it'll be for a while." On reaching for the phone to tell her in person, Detective Inspector Gerald Thomas entered the room. Glyn Davies, his sergeant, accompanied him.

Within four hours of the body being discovered, Detective Inspector Thomas had been called in from Wales Regional HQ. Before leaving, he distributed tasks that he felt able to delegate, sought and obtained authority to hand over much of his important casework to fellow officers, summoned his sergeant and driver (who were always on call), and picked up the bag he had kept packed, ready for the purpose.

With the introductions and formalities over, Thomas got straight down to business. He encouraged the constable to tell him what had been established to date.

"As much background as you can give me."

He turned to his sergeant.

"Usual form, please, Glyn—note anything useful."

Constable Baker outlined the few details that were known at the time.

The body, a male, had washed ashore in Darren's Cove, off Penryn Point. Hands and feet tied, it had been found by a couple of holidaymakers who, despite the terrible shock, had the presence of mind to run to the coastguard on the Point, who in turn phoned Constable Baker.

"Doctor Johns says it had been in the water for over a week," the constable stated. "He was naked."

"Why was the doctor naked?" interrupted a grinning Sergeant Davies.

"No, no... The doctor wasn't..." Constable Baker stopped himself too late.

"You'll have to excuse my sergeant," the Detective Inspector interjected quickly. "He has a warped sense of humour. Useful to break the ice sometimes, but not always appreciated." He glanced across at his sergeant with an admonishing look.

"Where's our body now?"

"I had it taken to the hospital at Bangor. There aren't any facilities around here. Managed to get a local bobby from Bangor to stay with it. He's under strict instruction not to let anyone near."

"Good. I'll get over there as soon as I can. Make sure no one gets near that body."

"Doctor Johns is the local doctor, I presume. Is he good? Can we rely on him?"

Constable Baker was taken aback at the thought of Philip Johns' integrity being questioned. "I have known the doctor a long time." The constable then answered both questions with a single positive answer: "Yes." He added, "His surgery is just over the road. I see him virtually every day."

"Did he carry out an examination?"

"No. Just preliminary. He said it was not his role. He'll be available when surgery has finished. I'll let him know you've arrived, shall I?"

"It's ok, my sergeant can do that. Thanks, Glyn."

Glyn nodded, indicating that he understood.

"Nothing to identify the body either then, if his clothes had been removed?"

"No."

"What was he tied with?"

"Looked like ordinary tape to me. Like masking tape, come to think of it."

"Masking tape wouldn't stay intact in the sea for a week, would it, Glyn?" the Detective Inspector asked his sergeant.

"Doubt it, sir, but the lab boys will establish the make and composition when we get to it."

The DI stood and stretched his arms.

"Let's focus on who he is, how he died, and how long he'd been in the water. Then maybe we can make some progress. Nationality - any ideas?"

"Couldn't say," Constable Baker replied. "He's white, that's about all I would say. Tall though, a good bit over six feet, maybe six three, six four, something like that. There are markings on his back and shoulders. Could be tattoos."

"Age?"

"About forty."

"Build?"

"Difficult to tell, but I'd say powerfully built."

"Have there been strangers around?"

"Not that I am aware of. I'll make enquiries."

"OK, that's your role from here, Owen. It is Owen, isn't it?"

"Yes, sir."

"Right, Owen, you can take that on board. You know the locals, the relevant people to ask, we don't. Start with shopkeepers, publicans, hotels, B&Bs, early risers, paperboys, the postman, farmers. You get the idea. I know it's a tall order—I'll get you some foot soldiers drafted in as soon as I can. Go to boatyards. Find out if anyone unusual has hired out a boat in the last few weeks or months. For that matter, get a list of all hirings over the same period. Anything else you can think of, or I should know?"

"Can't think of anything."

"Well," Thomas suggested, trying to be helpful and prompt the constable, "Do you have any reason to think there might be a Moelfre connection, or was our man just floating by, as it were?"

"Can't imagine a connection, sir."

"Then start imagining," interrupted Thomas. "Local villains? What about your usual clients? Anything there?"

"Not really. No one I would associate with murder. It's mostly petty crime around here."

"Thanks."

The Detective Inspector walked to the window and looked across the harbour, admiring the peace and the view.

"Glyn, when will the full team arrive?"

"I'll check." Sergeant Davies leaned across the desk. "All right to use this one?" he said, nodding toward the phone. "Not a shared line, is it?"

The constable confirmed it was safe to use. "Help yourself."

"What's the local strength, constable?" enquired Thomas.

"There's just me and one other."

"And where is this *one other*?"

"Constable Logan. He's at the Point—Peryn Point, sir, keeping everyone away until you get there."

"All right, all right," Thomas said forcefully, gaining everyone's attention by clapping his hands loudly together.

17

"Let's get on with it. This is a full-blown murder enquiry. We'll need more people on the ground. That's for certain." More questions came to mind, and again, the Detective Inspector turned to the unfortunate Constable Baker.

"Are we on a main shipping route?"

"Not any longer. Busy once, now it's mainly pleasure craft. This part of the coast is a boating paradise. That's why so many come."

"Lots of coves and bays? Hidden and remote?"

"Oh yes. Really beautiful."

"I'm sure they are. Any smuggling on a major scale? Drugs? People?" he asked, attempting to be more relevant.

"Don't think so. The Coast Guard being based here would be a definite deterrent."

"You think so? Thanks, constable."

"Sergeant, where's our lot? Any news?" Thomas asked, becoming a little agitated.

"All on the way. They are sending Donald Wearing to do the PM. He'll be leaving in about two hours."

"Owen, can you arrange a list of your tearaways for Sergeant Davies, please? Glyn, will you run them through the central computer for any previous? Also, any known contacts you may have missed?"

The constable scribbled down some names with addresses and agreed to pass the remainder over as soon as he could.

Doctor Johns tapped on the open door, announcing his arrival. He looked passively around the room.

"Owen, is this a good time?" he asked.

The interview with Doctor Johns took longer than Detective Inspector Thomas thought. As anticipated, the doctor was not able to throw any new light on the victim, nor could he express a view whether the man was likely to have died in any other way than the apparent drowning. The best he could do was to assume, for the time being at least, that the body had indeed been in the sea for at least a week. Also, to note some surprise at where it had emerged. He said it was very rare for anything to wash up in Darren's Cove. He did, however, give a far more detailed description of the body and scene than Constable Baker.

Thomas was not particularly surprised. He had learned nothing new about the murdered man and didn't really want guesswork at this important early stage. He was far more interested in what else the doctor had seen, or believed he had seen, as he ran down the cliff path leading to the beach. These were events which the doctor suggested "...were not spectacular but a bit odd. Unusual even."

Thomas made him go over it several times before he felt satisfied, and the doctor agreed to make himself available to meet again later that day.

The Detective Inspector was impressed with the man and said so. He nodded his thanks and reminded him that this was a murder enquiry and not to discuss it with anyone. He was hopeful that he may have been given his first lead. Constable Baker returned to the room.

"Is Peryn Point far?" Detective Inspector Thomas asked him. "I could do with a walk."

"Very easy to get to. Left out of here, to the end of the harbour and follow the path along the headland. It's signposted. We can be there in fifteen minutes."

"I'll go by myself, thanks. You'd better stay here. All sorts of people are coming. In fact, I'm surprised the press haven't arrived yet". Constable Baker's expression conveyed that he was not used to cases of this size involving the press. "Don't be so worried, a press officer is on her way. She'll sort them out. No statements or interviews of any sort. Refer everyone and everything to her. No exceptions, understood?"

The DI changed the subject.

"Constable, tell me. What is life like in Moelfre? I need to try and understand. Helps me see the, er, *differences*..." He let out the word very slowly.

"I always try to find the differences. Isn't that right, Glyn?"

"Yes, sir, you certainly do. You're always telling me to find the, er, differences."

"What are folk like in Moelfre, Owen? Help me understand."

Thomas pulled a chair from beneath the table and dragged it toward him. He motioned the constable to sit down.

"What do you mean? What can I tell you?"

"What type of people are they? Old, young? How do they spend their time? Make their money? Do they keep to themselves? Do they have orgies? When did you issue the last speeding ticket? Are they inquisitive? I appreciate your observations will be quite general, but believe me, it all helps. Come on, constable. What happens behind the curtains? This is your patch. Tell me about it. What constitutes normality? The everyday? Day-in, day-out life? Ordinary life?"

The Detective Inspector listened carefully, trying to build a picture of what was normal. So normal, in fact, that to all intents and purposes, it doesn't exist. No one ever sees it. This was always his starting point. The red, when it was usually blue; the visitor who always came on a Monday, but this week came on a Thursday. The shop closed when it was normally open. These were his *differences*—differences he needed to ease open the puzzle.

"Glyn, you'd better talk to the couple who found the body. Take them through what they saw on the beach. Then go and see the Coast Guard. Ask about tides and currents. See if it's possible, with the right sort of help, to establish where someone ending up here might have entered the water. Talk to Customs & Excise, Coast Guard HQ, and the Navy. Tell them to make their best experts available."

He took a moment to pause, then continued.

"Any problems, contact Commander Bill Peers at Admiralty House. He is an old friend, and he owes me a few favours. Haven't seen him for some months, but he may be able to point us in the right direction. Find out how easy it is to get lists of shipping routes, destinations, cargos—you know, the sort of thing—any unusual happenings. Ask him if records are kept and, more importantly, collated. Who keeps them?" As an afterthought, he added, "I know we don't know where our body is from yet, but Glyn, can you get someone to start checking out missing persons as soon as we get a proper description? There can't be that many six-foot-four-inch men missing, surely? Keep me posted."

Darren's Cove, he discovered, was charming. It formed a deep 'U' shape with steep-sided rock faces angled toward the sea. Breaks in the rocks created several cave-like openings where bathers could shelter from the incoming breeze. One side of the cove was longer and a more irregular shape than the other, and on this side, the beach was strewn with boulders as though some beneficent giant had casually sprinkled them the night before so children could climb and play amongst them. Seagulls and cormorants played in the wind, swooping, then soaring high, lifted above the top of the cliffs.

About fifteen onlookers gathered on the sandy beach, facing
Constable Logan. They watched as the DI approached.

"Detective Inspector Thomas," he said, showing the
constable his warrant card. "You are Constable Logan?"

"I am, sir."

"Where was the body found?"

"Just about there," he replied, pointing to a spot now
underwater. "The tide, you understand."

"Do you know if Doctor Johns examined it here, on the
beach, before it was removed? Were you present?"

"Yes, sir. He didn't have much time, though. The sea comes
in quickly here."

"Was the area undisturbed? Had anyone been walking all
over it?"

"I don't think so, but I can't be sure. I arrived within ten,
maybe fifteen minutes of receiving the call from Owen—er,
Constable Baker. Nothing obvious, though."

Thomas told the constable to stay until the forensic experts
arrived.

Doctor Johns arrived as arranged, and before long, he and
Thomas were locked in earnest discussion before making
their way up the hill path. About a third of the way up,
Constable Logan noticed the doctor pointing across the cove
but couldn't quite make out at precisely what. Interestingly,
on his way back to the beach, the Detective Inspector idly
observed that the doctor must have taken a different route.

For the moment, however, he dismissed this thought and took time to reflect. He stood perfectly still and took a deep breath, filling his lungs with the fresh salt air. The views were stunning, and the echoing sound of the gulls in flight reminded him of his childhood—a magical moment from a long-ago memory. It was immediately obvious to him why anyone would choose to live here. "And", he thought, "Not a bad place to die either." On the other hand, he countered, "Nowhere is a good place to end up murdered."

He slowly walked back the way he came, along the path across the headland, past the harbour wall, and into the station. He was feeling more on top of things.

"Come on, sergeant," he said. "We've got a lot of work to do. Rest period over. You can drive me to the hospital—it's time to take a look at that body. He paused and then changed his tone. "You may also want to make some arrangements on the home front. We could be here on this case for quite a while." He was aware that Sergeant Davies had only been married for four months. "I know," he said. "Tough life, isn't it? Easy to miss your, shall we say, home comforts. But just think how pleased she'll be to have you back. Look at me, I'm delighted to be away for a few weeks." He smiled. "Suggest you give her a call—use the phone in there. But be quick, OK?"

Watching him close the door and pick up the phone, he spoke under his breath. "Who says Detective Inspectors don't have any heart?"

Sergeant Davies returned to the car, opened the rear door for his DI, climbed in himself, checked the police road map for the most direct route, put the engine in gear, and headed away. In turn, Thomas was reassembling the facts learnt that day, beginning to shape possible scenarios in order of plausibility. He then set about working out the best approach for each so the inquiry proper could start in the morning. Content, he leaned forward, making eye contact in the car mirror.

"We need to find a decent place to stay. Preferably somewhere that serves good beer. Give Owen a ring and ask him which pub serves the best pint, will you?"

He sat back again. "Glyn," he said, "This is really not going to be an easy one, not by a long way." He then slapped his driver on the back. "But cheer up, the first couple of rounds are on me..."

CHAPTER THREE
Hidden Truths

Central London.

It was Deputy Controller David Stewart's birthday. He was fifty-eight, his intense life more than leaving its mark. Removing his clasped hands from behind his head, he picked up the grey file placed down a little earlier, swung his feet across the corner of the desk and flicked through the pages until he found what he was searching for. After a few minutes of intense reading, he inhaled deeply, then exhaled with slow elaboration. The air passed his lips, becoming a slow whistle. "Well, well," he said aloud. His mind focused.

Has the time come? To tell the controller the whole truth?

He fixed his gaze out of the window, pondering not only the risks, but the consequences he was facing.

No. I am not ready. I am too close. Nothing must derail this.

He therefore took his time to ensure his story was in order before calling the Controller.

'C'—as he preferred to be known—listened carefully and without interruption. David briefed him, to the extent he was prepared to, spelling out the seriousness of the looming implications of a Russian Agent's body being discovered on UK shores.

"You'd better come over," the controller fumed. "Give me half an hour to clear my desk."

Situated in the same building, David left his office and opted not to take the lift, instead climbing the stairs to the fourth floor. An initially uncertain smile greeted him as he entered the outer room.

"I haven't seen you for a while," said the duty officer. "You have been missed. Go straight in, he is expecting you."

The Controller straightaway looked up from his desk. "How the hell did we allow this to happen? Why didn't we know? Why didn't I know?" He let out a series of expletives that David had seldom used or heard since he left the forces. "It's a..."

"...gigantic cock-up," agreed David, playing along.

Remembering his position and status, the Controller forced himself to breathe more easily and pointed to the decanter on an occasional table between two well-worn wingback, pitted leather chairs. "Pour me a whisky, would you?" then added as an afterthought, "Have one yourself. It's a special one—grown, brewed, distilled, savoured, and worshipped in my hometown. Best blend, twelve years in the making."

David declined. "Need to keep a clear head, a lot going on," choosing to remain completely in control given his precarious position.

The Controller re-read and signed the papers before him, stamping them 'Internal Only'. With his emotions now back in check, he picked up the phone and spoke into it. "Person-to-person delivery, please. Thanks."

He replaced the receiver, stepped from behind his desk, and shook David's hand.

David's normally unflappable demeanour told C what he already knew—the situation was real and urgent. Only David knew it was deliberate.

"Local or international implications?" the controller asked.

"Both." David replied.

"That bad."

"Worse."

David's team by now included Doctor Johns, recently recruited to be his man in Moelfre. To confirm that the body of Alexi Gregoriof, known to MI6 under the code name *Lonestar*, had been found washed up, then to manage things locally from there. The local police force was investigating, but it wouldn't take them long to establish who the body was. Or its significance. Whilst a full-blown murder investigation had already started, so far, it was just a body on the beach. Not even the Controller had full insight into David's strategy to unmask the mole.

"How long do you think we have before the fan hits the proverbial?" the Controller asked.

"Maybe a day, maybe two. Maybe a week," David replied.

"We can't rely on that," C added.

David noticed the Controller's usual calm expression had changed. Almost imperceptibly, just for a second or two. But he noticed.

The Controller slowly made his way back to his desk. Taking time to think, he picked up the phone. "Julie," he asked, "Has the letter I gave you been delivered? No? That's all right. Don't worry. I need to make a couple of changes, that's all. Thanks."

He looked carefully at his Deputy. "Is your doctor reliable? Can we slow down the local inquiry? It's on your head. It's your team. See what you can do."

C is distancing himself already, David thought. *No bad thing at all.* The Controller walked from behind his desk, unlocked the safe, and took out a small leather-bound book, which he placed in the inner pocket of his jacket. He closed and locked the safe, turned to David, and said, "I want you to keep this between us until I have had time to brief up the line. Before things get completely out of hand. Come on, come with me." He opened the door to the adjoining office, where Julie Summers handed him the sealed letter, and they walked along the panelled corridor to the operations room.

CHAPTER FOUR
Doctor Johns

Anglesey, North Wales.

Detective Inspector Thomas called his team together for the 8 a.m. morning briefing. He strode into the room and, in his usual fashion, clapped his hands loudly. "All right, all right. That's not applause, you lot. Less noise, please. Quieten down." He paused, then continued over the reducing chatter. "That's better. Now let me introduce Inspector Stonely. He is taking over the..."

"*Assisting,*" the new inspector interrupted.

"*Assisting* the enquiry," repeated the DI, glancing over with a smile.

"The national press has hold of this now. You all know a press officer has been appointed, but be warned, be alert, be on your guard. These people are skilled at ferreting out information. It's their job. And your job is not to let them. Refer everyone to the press officer. Warn your family, friends, and neighbours to be extra careful. All understood?" He scanned the room for confirmations.

"Now then, Inspector Stonely. Over to you."

Inspector Stonely stepped forward and took over.

"Any news on identifying the body?"

"Not yet," volunteered Constable Barnes. "No one of his description has been reported missing locally or in the UK."

30

"Follow that up. Keep on it. Talk to colleagues in Europe. There can't be many six-foot-four males who haven't turned up for their morning constitutional. Get authority for TV broadcasts. Speak to the press office. Let's use them for a change. We need to find out who he is. Any significance with the tattoos? Do they tell us anything about possible background?"

"All underway," Constable Jennings confirmed.

"Good. That's a start, at least. Anything from the door-to-door enquiries? Who's talking to the locals?" He looked around the room.

"Jennings, that's also you, isn't it? Any joy?"

"No luck there either," Constable Jennings replied.

"No luck? You are supposed to be experienced police officers! We need some answers. Someone must have seen something. Talk to Constable Baker. I've met him - he seems to know who's who and what's what in the area. Where are we with local shipping? Nationality? Has the cause of death been established yet?"

Inspector Stonely stopped and again looked around.

"I have heard good things about this unit, let's keep that reputation going. Leave it with you. Oh, and I'll be relocating to this building from tomorrow. As they say in the best movies, my door is always open."

Detective Inspector Thomas re-took the floor.

"You heard what the man said. Let's get on with it—a busy day ahead. Back here eight-thirty tomorrow morning."

At that moment, the desk sergeant entered the room and spoke quietly into Thomas's ear.

"Doctor Johns is here. He said you asked him to come in."

"I don't recall asking him—I must be slipping. Never mind. Give me ten minutes to finish here, then show him to my office. Thanks."

"Ask Doctor Johns to come through, would you?"

The doctor came into the room and sat down.

"Good to see you, doctor. Do you have something you want to tell me, or is it purely a social call? I'm assuming it's to do with our murder. Or do you know something about my health that I don't?"

Doctor Johns didn't smile. Nor answer.

"I had it on my list to call on you today. You have saved me a visit," continued Thomas. "The last time we met, you told me of your journey back to your surgery after examining the body on the beach. Can you run it past me again? If I remember correctly, you saw someone leave the area where the body was found. Quite a way away to be certain who it was, but I am now guessing close enough to be about to tell me? Or am I wrong?" He looked straight into the doctor's eyes. "I sensed then that you knew something."

32

The Detective Inspector took the doctor's unrelenting stare and silence as agreement. He went further.

"If I am right, we'll deal with it confidentially. I'll take care of you. And I'll try to ignore the fact that withholding information is a criminal offence. Are you being threatened, blackmailed, or what?"

"No, I'm not being blackmailed. But yes, I am involved. Though not in the way you are thinking. I have come to ask for your help."

He continued looking directly at the Detective Inspector. "As one professional to another, I am here to ask you to slow down the enquiry. But I am not at liberty to tell you why." He paused.

"I can tell you this request has come from the highest level."

"Go on," said Thomas, "You have my attention."

"That authority is fully aware of who your body is and the circumstances of his death."

Detective Inspector Thomas had been in the force a long time and thought he was long past being shocked. He was, however, totally taken aback.

"What the devil are you talking about? What authority? Whose authority? I am a police officer. I could and should arrest you for this. A man has been brutally killed, and there's a full-scale murder investigation underway. You'd better explain yourself. And quickly."

Doctor Johns leaned back in his chair. "Listen," he said, "I know this must be confusing for you. I also know you are well regarded by your superiors and colleagues alike. From what I have established, you are judged to be in the file marked 'Not Corruptible.' Loyal." He lowered his voice. "Can you see that it's precisely because you can be trusted that I am speaking to you so openly?"

"I ask you again," the DI said slowly. "Who are you, and what on earth are you trying to say? Why are you ferreting around finding things out about me? You'd better speak up, and it had better be good. Who do you represent? What higher authority? Are you even a doctor? You turn up in my office with some cock-and-bull story asking me—telling me—to ease off on a murder enquiry."

"I'm not at liberty to say," Doctor Johns replied. "You'll have to trust me. What's your instinct?"

"My instinct is irrelevant. My experience, though, tells me everything I need to know. And it's telling me not to believe a single word. Even though I can't think of a reason why you would make up such a ridiculous story."

The Detective Inspector moved from behind his desk and stood between Doctor Johns and the door.

"I'm afraid that won't do, doctor. That won't do at all. I remind you again that this is a murder enquiry. And you are withholding information. What's *your* instinct about that?"

The doctor didn't speak.

"Give me something tangible to go on. I'll check it out and go from there."

"Gaining time," the doctor said, "Is the essence here. Believe me, this is no simple cops-and-robbers or straightforward murder. If this goes wrong, the consequences are international." Leaning forward, the Detective Inspector spoke firmly and with deliberate measure.

"I very much suggest you stay here until I get back."

Thomas left the room and caught sight of his sergeant leaving the building. He opened the window and called him back.

"Sorry, Philip, I can't let you go just yet. We're either on to something big—really big—or I'm losing my grip, which is quite possible in this job. I need you to stay with the doctor and prevent him from leaving. Keep him busy. Show him your family photographs. Tell him anything. The trouble you have with your feet—you tell me often enough. Puncture his tyre. Put a trace on the phone, find out who he has spoken to. He's in my room now and I need to know everything he does. I can't arrest him just now, but we need him to stay where he is. I'll be gone for a few hours. Thanks, Philip."

He drove quickly to the modest inner-terrace house of his long-retired former boss. Now living in idyllic mid-Wales, Thomas rang the bell several times impatiently. He was met by a smiling but now lined elderly face.

35

"Gerald, what a lovely surprise. It's been a while." He gripped Thomas's arm for balance and shook his hand. "Come in. What brings you here?" They made their way to the sitting room. Thomas mentioned he was sorry he hadn't been in touch for a long time but otherwise brushed aside polite convention.

"It's not a social call, I'm afraid, I need your help. Remember the backroom boys you were close to in Whitehall? I don't have much time for explanation, but I need a name— someone you trust."

"What have you got yourself into? It must be important for you to come to an old campaigner like me."

"You'll have to trust me," he remarked, remembering he had heard that phrase already today. "I give you my word. I won't involve you in any way."

"That important, eh?" Edward Cox eased himself from his chair and made his way into his office. He returned a few minutes later and handed Thomas a slip of paper on which he had written a name and telephone number.

"Remember it," he said sharply. "You'll find it helpful." Thomas committed it to memory and handed the slip back. Edward promptly pushed the paper into the burning living room fire until he was satisfied it was totally consumed. The Detective Inspector thanked Edward, shook his hand, and left.

Edward Cox waved goodbye and watched as the car raced away. Then, picking up his phone, he slowly dialled.

"He will be ringing you any time now," he said carefully.

"That's fine," said the voice at the end of the line. "You did the right thing. Treat yourself to a drink. I am going to pour myself a whisky. Relax, I will take it from here."

Thomas glanced at his watch. He had already used up much of his limited time and hoped his sergeant was keeping the doctor entertained. He stretched through the car window and fixed the flashing blue light on the roof, driving a little too recklessly through the crowded streets.

"Out of the way!" he shouted, gesticulating at the slow-moving vehicles.

He spotted a public phone box, slammed on the brakes, stopped the car, and ran toward it.

"Chances are it won't be working," he thought, "But worth a try."

As improbable as it seemed to him, the seed planted in his head by Doctor Johns was beginning to grow, flowering into the increasing possibility that the doctor could be right. Moreover, this could be a call way beyond his pay grade. Until he was more certain, he decided using the normal phone line was unwise and perhaps even risky. He needed to speak urgently to the contact Edward Cox had given him.

With the phone box door now hastily pulled open, he picked up the phone, pushed in several coins, and dialled.

"Exports Section," the voice eventually said. "How can I help you?"

"Would you put me through to Charles Brocton?"

"Who should I say is calling? Is he expecting your call?"

"Tell him, Detective Inspector Gerald Thomas from Wales Regional HQ. It's urgent."

"Can I ask who recommended you to us and the reason for your call?"

"It's police business. And..." pausing to emphasise the point, "...it's of the utmost importance."

"Very well. One moment, please."

The phone crackled to life.

"I've been expecting your call, Mr Thomas. Come and see me."

CHAPTER FIVE
Higher Powers

Warrens St David, North Wales.

Detective Inspector Thomas left the dark, dreary, and altogether anonymous building. He desperately needed some time to assimilate the extraordinary events of the day before returning to Moelfre. Making a slight detour, he swerved off the main road and headed towards Warrens St David. He parked as close as he could to the sea, walked a hundred feet, stepped onto the beach, and breathed in the glorious fresh air. The beach was all but deserted. *What the hell is going on?* It was approaching dusk. Light was giving way to the approaching dark of evening as he walked unhurriedly over the damp sand. After his meeting with Charles Brocton, he knew his involvement was now total. His day had begun like any other —as far as any day is normal in a murder enquiry- but now, it made no sense whatsoever. Although Brocton had told him very little, he knew it was sufficient to run with the doctor's story for a little longer yet. He had to make a decision. If it was true, then he needed to know how deep it went. His mind raced. "Who else knew? How high up the ranks did it go? After all, before today, Doctor Johns had been, well, just a doctor." He struggled to switch off. "Am I being set up? Am I being used in a covert operation?"

Finally, he regained some control. "This is all a bit far-fetched, to say the least. Or is it?" The wind across the bay was becoming stronger. It loosened the sand on the beach and pulled at his coat. "Come on," he said to himself. "Get a grip. The mysterious doctor awaits."

Sergeant Davies was by now running out of inspiration. In the past, it had been said he could win competitions involving speaking for hours without saying anything, and it had once even been mischievously suggested that he become an MP. At the same time, Doctor Johns was, perhaps unsurprisingly, agitated to the point of being ready to explode as Thomas entered the room.

"Thanks, sergeant. You'd better get home. Apologise to your good lady for me."

"Made your enquiries, Detective?" the doctor asked bluntly. Thomas waited for his sergeant to leave the room, closed the door, and turned to Doctor Johns.

"You surely wouldn't expect me to do any less."

"And your conclusions?"

"I'm not going to take anything further until you open up and tell me more. If you do, I'll play my part, but I need more. The when, the what, the why, and, of course, the *who*."

"Good," replied the doctor.

"I can tell you some, but not all."

He again confirmed that he was acting with the knowledge and authority of those at the highest level.

"The people I represent are involved with matters beyond borders and beyond what you and I might consider normal rules of decency. There is no longer such a thing as fair play, if indeed there ever was—the world has moved on. The opposition does not play by the old rules, so neither, it seems, do we. Rules that protect us all: your safety, my safety, the safety of us all. They stoop to depths that you and I cannot fathom. I am simply a messenger." Then, articulating each word very deliberately, he added in unambiguous tone—a tone that you knew was meant:

"You cannot discuss or inform anyone of *anything* I'm about to tell you... Is that understood?"

Thomas listened with begrudging but growing admiration as the doctor outlined only what was strictly relevant and necessary as background information. He was becoming increasingly convinced, though still without a shred of evidence or logic, that the doctor was who he said he was. A man, he thought, who not only cared for the health and well-being of his patients but for the health, well-being, and safety of his country. He knew at that moment he was not only heavily involved, but he was about to join the doctor in whatever came next.

"I will do what needs to be done," he reassured the doctor.

"Excellent."

They looked at each other, the balance of power now shifted. "First, we need to slow down the murder inquiry. Not cease it entirely yet, just slow it down. After all, we know who did it. It's really a waste of public money, but my people need more time to deal with matters at their end. Now you are onboard, I will start that process now."

Doctor Johns picked up the phone and dialled the number for Deputy Controller David Stewart. There was a quiet, brief conversation that the DI could not quite hear, though he caught the gist of it. The doctor placed the receiver down, shook Thomas's hand, and left, saying he would be back directly.

Within the hour, Inspector Stonely came into the room and said, "I'm sorry, Gerry. I've just received a call from London. I've been put on another case. They only want you on this one. You've got my number if you need me. Keep in touch."

"Yes, of course. Heavy stuff. Good luck," Thomas replied, inwardly expressing genuine shock at the speed of events and the influence of whoever Doctor Johns had spoken to. He deliberated how best to deal with it now. He needed to keep the formal investigation alive, but until he heard more from the doctor, he needed time. It was approaching 10 p.m., so Thomas decided he could do no more for the day and planned to set the ball rolling again at the 8:30 a.m. briefing the following morning.

CHAPTER SIX
Duplicity

Malta.

Following the shooting of Jack, David Stewart used the period to good effect at his Malta retreat. He needed a break and a chance to reflect. He had to unwind and then rewind as he began thinking the unthinkable.

He spent two months in the serenity of his temporary surroundings, which served only to reinforce its contrast with the dreadful, life-shortening business he was in and the sheer duplicity and mercilessness of the life he was leading. After all, he was, at heart, he thought, a decent human being. How Kim Philby slept peacefully and easily at night, if indeed he ever slept at all, David could not imagine. Then he asked himself, "Am I that different from him? Who is right and who is wrong?"

His mind filtered back to his time in Effos in Greece, from walking on the beach with Jannine. She looked so innocent, alluring, and irresistible. He was aware she was the conduit, the honeytrap that had been set for him. He also played his part, reckoning that sooner or later, she would lead him to the nest and the Queen Bee.

Effos, in Greece, particularly the Square at Lagaria, with its meandering courtyards and mellow stonework, had stunning views. No one knew with absolute certainty why it had been chosen. There was no speculation, little curiosity—just an easy, carefree acceptance far beyond the bounds of naivety. It was, quite simply, how it was.

It was not the most central of the three squares by quite a distance. Nor was it the easiest to reach on foot. It lay on the wilder, western side of the coast, at a point where the sea did not kiss and gently caress the shore as it did in Effos Bay, nor invite play and passion as at Xreoss Bay. Instead, it relentlessly smashed into the jagged outcrop, seemingly intent on smoothing the rough edges to make life sweeter for the people of the village.

The violence of action, it was often said, was merely the sea's frustration over a poor summer crop, a disappointing catch, or perhaps even the hurt of a broken heart—pain that was taken away, scolded, and then swept back, finally lost in the cascading, smothering spray.

On some rare and wonderful days, when the wind blew in a caring direction, Lagaria Square gathered cool, comforting sea breezes that teasingly wrapped around the white tablecloths and awnings of the neat cafes before generously sharing with its charges a refreshing flourish of spirit—one that reflected the very essence of the village.

Every day felt special in Effos, but on Fridays—when the sun, having driven away the clouds, shone at its brightest—village life was presented more eloquently than words could ever convey.

Friday meant that all work in the village stopped. By midday, those who could—the young and the old, those seeking love, widows lonely yet hopeful, dreamers—gathered by the open-fronted bakeries, bars, and cafes surrounding Lagaria's faded marble fountain.

Friday brought the precious sense of the security of home. Even the sea and the wind played their part in making Effos special to the people who cherished it. To belong to the village meant being safe and feeling safe. It meant knowing that nothing would harm those it protected within the embrace of the mountains and its outstretched valley arms. Every Friday felt like this to Jannine for as long as she could remember.

She leaned across the table.

"A little more wine?" she asked, tilting the bottle invitingly toward her companion's glass. Her head was slightly angled, and her lips parted just enough to reveal the perfect white of her teeth. Her blue-grey eyes smiled directly into his as she laughed, fully aware of the effect she was having. She was playing with him, teasing and flirting all at the same time. When she looked at someone that way, she was irresistible—save for the most world-weary and insensitive.

45

"Do you think they will ever return?" Jannine posed the question in a sombre tone.

"Everyone returns to Effos sooner or later," he reassured her. "Like you, it's so beautiful here." He gently pulled her hand toward him and kissed it, his eyes never leaving hers. It was his turn to be mischievous. "It's so still, so calm, so peaceful. Shall we walk? The wine will keep."

In the bay beyond the far edge of the square, a group of fishermen pulled the boat from the shallow water onto the shingle. Jannine watched as it fell onto its side, where it would remain until the next day's fishing. Each fisherman greeted Jannine warmly as they passed on their way to the square.

"Any luck?" she asked. "Good catch?"

"Not today. The fish were too clever for us. Tomorrow will be different."

"Tomorrow. Always tomorrow," laughed another.

As they strolled, Jannine allowed her thoughts to stray back. She looked at him intently, tugged at his arm, and turned him toward her.

"Some say you were involved."

"You shouldn't listen to such talk," he replied softly.

"Were you involved? Did you know?"

"I know many things. People tell me lots of things. But why does it interest you so much?"

"If you know all you claim to, you'll know the answer to that as well, won't you?" she laughed.

Jannine knew that her companion did indeed know. She had been told the night it happened. She also knew his real identity. He joined in with her laughter and draped his arm around her shoulder.

"Today is not for such serious talk. Let's walk a little more. We should head back—you did offer me wine, remember?" They turned and walked slowly back, hand in hand, but each lost in their own thoughts.

For the two months in Malta, there was seldom a day when David did not think about his time with Jannine. Or about Jannine. This was made easier by the absolute, blissful quiet. The only barely audible sound was that of the beating wings of birds as they greeted the morning, then soared and swooped in search of their first food of the day. Some mornings, it was so still that you could hear the gentle rustling of animals scurrying away from the rapidly approaching daylight.

He would run to the beach and dive into the rolling waves that crashed endlessly onto the boulder-strewn shore, taking the precious time needed to regain and rebalance his thoughts before making his next move in the international chess game—a game in which any wrong decision could, and probably would, be the last he would ever make.

47

"Three moves," he said aloud, "And it's checkmate."

He was sure he knew the answer. Now, he just needed the proof.

David forced his mind back to the task at hand and took advantage of the respite from the now-slower Moelfre inquiry. That gave him space to plan his next move. Scarcely weeks earlier, he had arranged for the removal of Alexi Gregoriof after learning he had been turned and was working for the other side. David was careful to ensure he was the only one, apart from his trusted team, who knew. He had recruited Doctor Johns as the latest member and arranged for Alexi's body to be washed up in Moelfre. The question the Deputy Controller was now asking himself was, "Who was the figure the doctor saw in the distance walking away from where the body was found? Who was the traitor in his house? What had he missed?"

This was a game in which loyalty was taken for granted, and although betrayal was, thankfully, very rare, it did happen. David reflected on Alexi's treachery and blamed himself for recruiting him. He had established beyond doubt that it had to be one of two people, and the time was nearing when he could keep his promise to Jack. He was so close that it was the moment to return to London. There were final tasks to be done.

After arriving at Heathrow, David took a taxi to his central London apartment, poured a beer and fell into the arms of fitful sleep. He woke early, arrived at his office by 8 a.m. and instructed his staff he was not to be disturbed. After locking the door, David then spent the next several hours ploughing through office files, personnel files, encrypted messages, telephone recordings, recruitment processes and references, searching for just one mistake—one fact that had been overlooked.

Then, all of a sudden, it came. He *had it*.

Malta had given David the vital space he needed to check his growing certainty about who the traitor was. He had held the thought in his mind for some time by now and savoured the promise he made to himself the day Jack was killed—the day Jack had been about to give him a name.

His thoughts took him back to a series of lectures entitled 'Best Practice Basic Police Work' by his first boss, Detective Sergeant Wistance, twenty years ago. "Look to the differences," he heard the DS say. The red when normally blue. The differences that are so small, no one sees them." "*Of course*," he said to himself, "It's so obvious, we never saw it. Thank you. God bless you, Walter Wistance."

CHAPTER SEVEN
Betrayal Unmasked

Central London.

Deputy Controller David Stewart walked the familiar route to the fourth floor and entered the outer office. George Robbins, the duty officer, greeted him.

"Is C available for a brief chat?" David asked.

"I'll check," said Robbins, a little startled at the sight of three unfamiliar police officers following David through the door. He returned a moment later.

"Yes, he is. Go through."

"Come in, David," C said. "Are you any closer to sorting this mess out? I have to meet the Minister at nine a.m."

"You'd be wise to avoid meeting the Minister or anyone else at the moment," David said.

"And in answer to your question," he added, "I couldn't be closer."

The Controller was about to explore this further when David's demeanour became even more serious, and he interjected.

"I need to say I haven't been completely honest with you, sir, and I may have to answer for that. But would you mind stepping into your outer office?"

C looked disconcerted as they walked toward the door.

"What's going on, David?"

David was no longer in a mood to discuss directly with the Controller. He was now staring intently at the traitor.

"I have suspected you for a while. You worked hand in hand with your collaborator Alexi Gregoriof and panicked when you heard his body had washed up in Moelfre. You were the figure who the doctor saw in the distance, walking away from where the body was found. You needed to check that it was Alexi's body—you needed to be certain. But you were too late. Doctor Johns was already there. I brought him on board to buy us time. Time to prove that Jannine was working for you. You wanted me gone in Greece, like Jack in Germany, but Jannine—your agent—led us to you. The honey trap failed. Your communications were intercepted and gave the game away. I've checked them myself. You didn't trust her, and not for the first time, you became anxious, sending at all hours, at unauthorised times. These differences made all the difference. I would understand if you believed what you were doing would keep the balance of power; there is merit in that, but as outdated as it is, loyalty is precious, loyalty between allies, nation to nation, man to wife, person to person.

You have betrayed this country, a country that has given you a safe and decent way of life, a home, and the freedom to say what you think and be who you are. Your worst crime is that you betrayed a good man. You were the mole who lured Jack Davenport to his death. He was my friend, and I will delight *in seeing you hang*."

51

"Superintendent…" David said formally, "Arrest that man," pointing at George Robbins, the desk duty officer.

Epilogue

"Did anyone work out who it was?" David Winters asked, looking around the room. The fire in the hearth had all but burned itself out, and the children were transfixed by both the story and the revelation.

"Come on, your taxi is here. It's late and chilly outside, so coats on and wrap up warm."

He stood by the door, watching them walk along the driveway, when one of the older children, still deep in thought, quietly spoke above the sounds of the night.

"Was that story true, Grandad? *Was* it you?"

David looked at him with kind eyes that gave nothing away.

"What do you think?"

He smiled, waved them goodbye, went back inside the house, and closed the door. He smiled again at a faded but cherished photograph of Jannine as the taxi drove away.

THE END

I will tell you where the taxi went next - if you join me for tea next Friday.

Acknowledgements

My family.

My mum and dad, still.

My writing partner, my boy, Stu.

www.ingramcontent.com/pod-product-compliance
Lightning Source LLC
Chambersburg PA
CBHW020320150626
46552CB00022B/3026